Only One Toy Allowed

Only One Toy Allowed
A Story for the Abandoned Children's Toys Project
by Sharon Ottenbreit
illustrations by Leslie Walden
Lulu.com, Raleigh, NC 2010

Summary: A teddy bear is abandoned when the little girl who owns him becomes homeless and can bring only one toy with her to the shelter. This book also includes a fund-raising idea for schools and churches to help the homeless.

ISBN 978-0-557-36426-8

Proceeds from the sale of this book will go to homeless shelters.

This book is dedicated to the children and adults who are without homes and with special appreciation to Detroit Friends Meeting.

My name is Teddy and I'm a toy.

You might think the life of a toy is wonderful.
It used to be wonderful,
but not today.

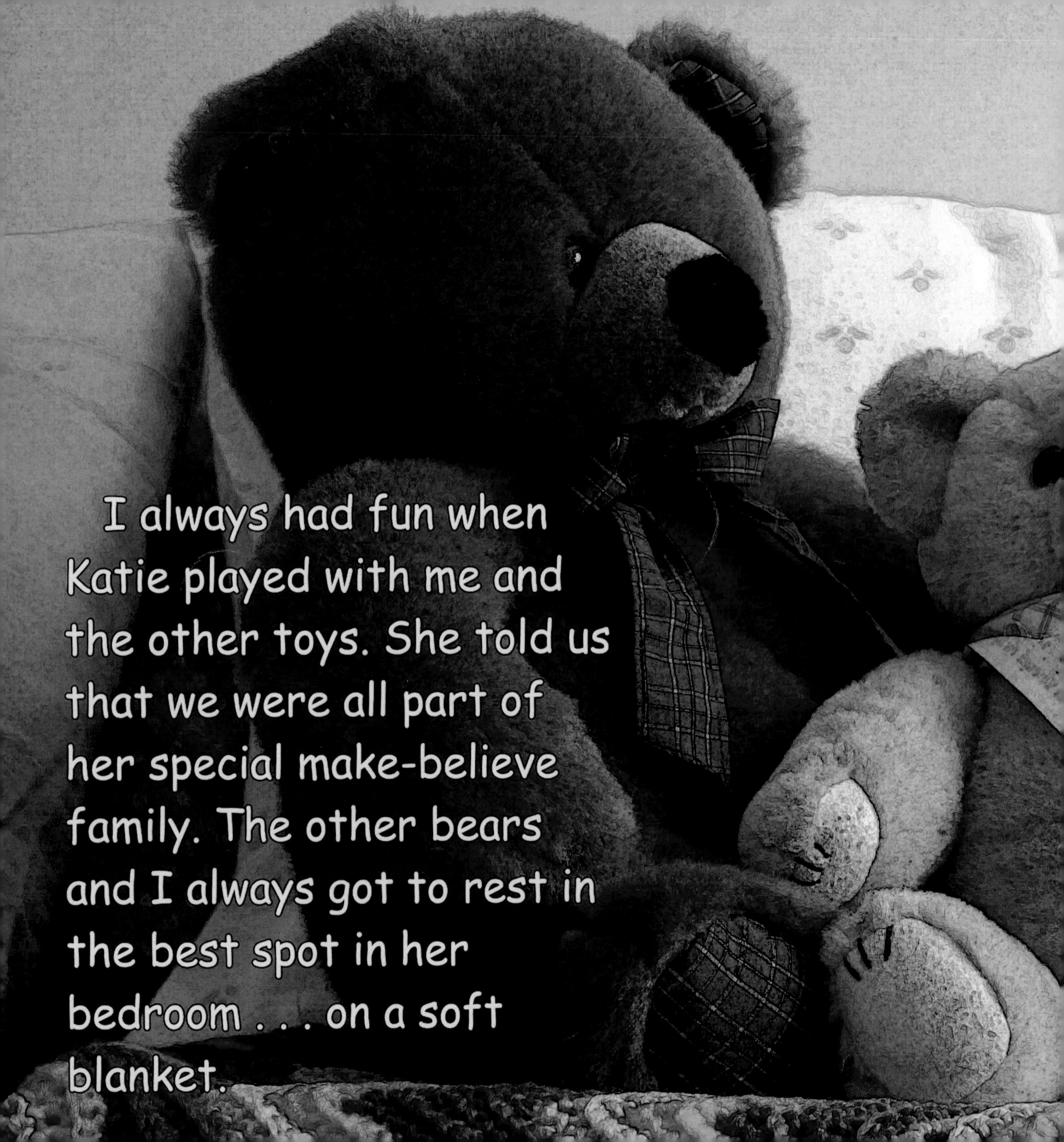

I always had fun when Katie played with me and the other toys. She told us that we were all part of her special make-believe family. The other bears and I always got to rest in the best spot in her bedroom . . . on a soft blanket.

All of the toys would wait patiently for Katie to come home from school. She usually came home in the late afternoon. I was hoping that today she would have the time to play with us again. We always had so much fun together!

As I looked out of the window, I could see the snow lying on the ground and the gray clouds floating high up in the sky. Darkness was starting to fall across the bedroom walls. The house had been darker lately. The lights must have stopped working.

It was four o'clock and I could hear Katie come into the house. I knew just what she would do. Just like every other day, I expected her to take off her coat, run up the stairs, throw open the door, and jump on her mattress that was on the floor.

But today was different. She did not come running up the stairs. The door was not thrown open. The mattress was not jumped on.

What could be wrong? What was taking her so long?

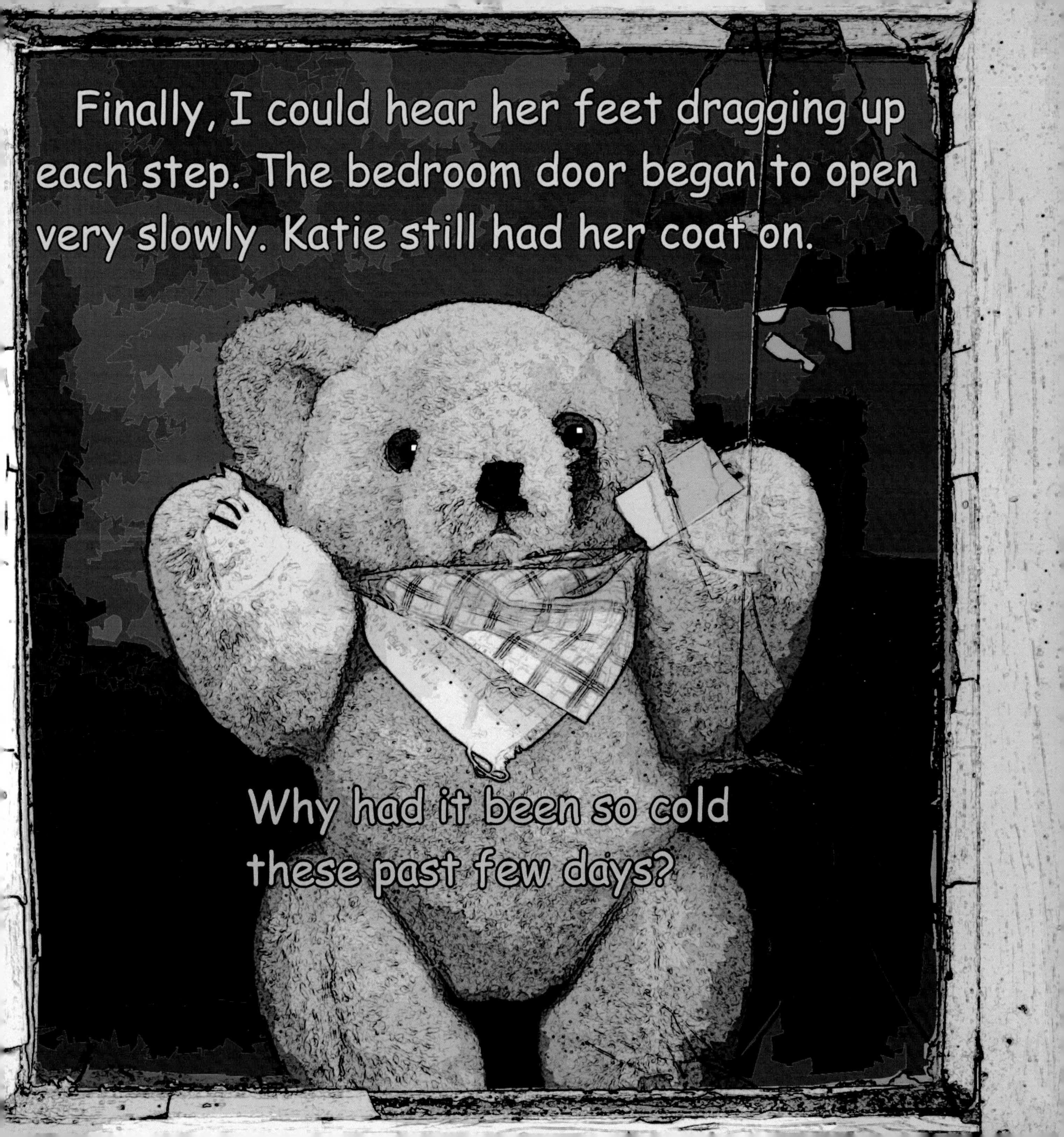
Finally, I could hear her feet dragging up each step. The bedroom door began to open very slowly. Katie still had her coat on.
Why had it been so cold these past few days?

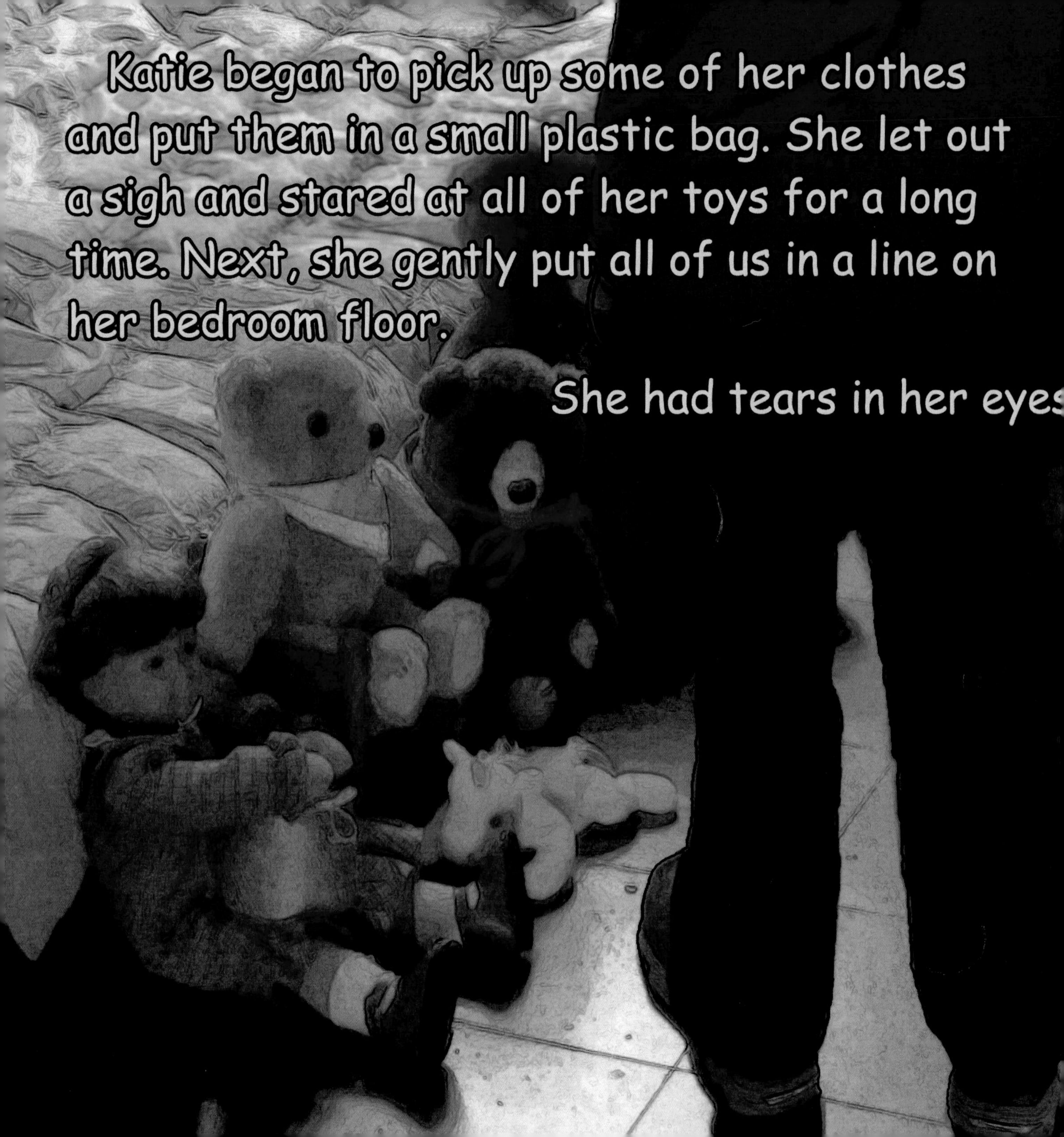

Katie began to pick up some of her clothes and put them in a small plastic bag. She let out a sigh and stared at all of her toys for a long time. Next, she gently put all of us in a line on her bedroom floor.

She had tears in her eyes

Katie picked me up and placed me in her arms along with the doll her grandma had given her. Then the three of us slowly walked out of her bedroom and down the stairs to the kitchen.

Where were we going?

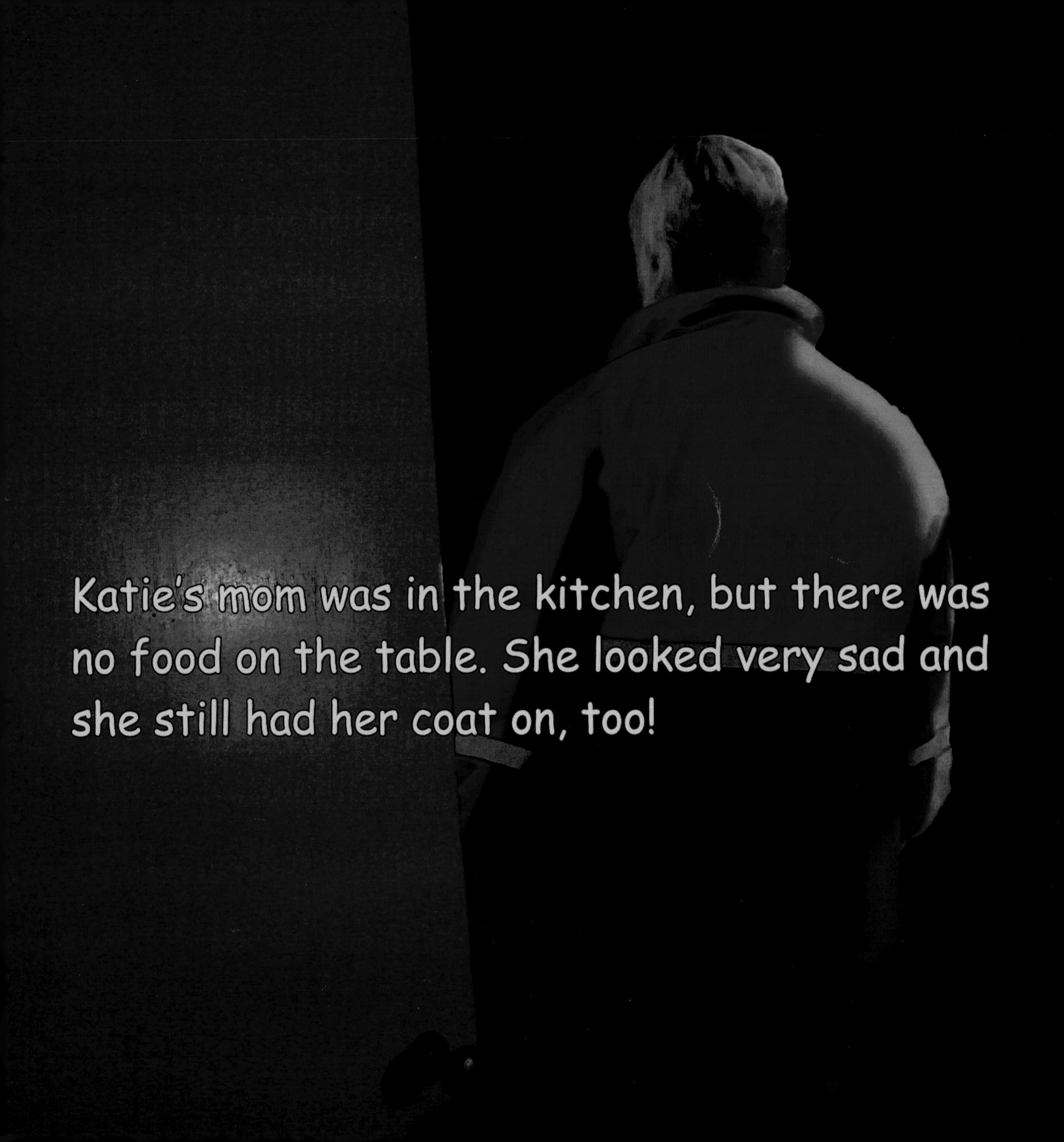

Katie's mom was in the kitchen, but there was no food on the table. She looked very sad and she still had her coat on, too!

The house was getting dark and all I could see was a candle dimly lighting the room.

Suddenly, someone blew out the candle.

The front door opened and I was being carried outside by Katie.

She held me tight as she turned around to take a long look at our home.

I was getting scared because there was a strange silence as we climbed into the car. When we began to drive down the street, Katie's mom said we had to leave our home because she didn't have money to pay for the water, or the lights, or the heat. She said we were homeless now.

WHAT DID THAT MEAN,

HOMELESS?

It was a long ride and I was so tired. The car finally stopped and we got out.

Katie's mom took her hand and we all walked into a big building that I had never seen before.

HOMELESS
SHELTER
INTAKE

As we went inside the building, a lady with a kind smile came up to us and talked in a very soft voice. I couldn't hear what she was saying, but somehow I trusted her.

She told us about the rules of this new home. Each child could only bring three outfits to wear and one toy to play with, because there wasn't much room.

Katie's mom said that this was where we would be living now. We had nowhere else to go.

I could feel Katie hugging me tighter. She cried out, "I can only bring one toy, Teddy. I'm sorry, but I have to keep the doll that Grandma gave me."

Katie leaned over and whispered in my ear,
"Tell our story, Teddy. Someone might help us."

After looking at me with
loving eyes, Katie
s...l...o...w...l...y
let go of my paw and
set me in a large
cardboard box
on top of some
other toys I
had never seen
before.

That was the last time I saw her, but I knew deep down in my heart that Katie would always love me.

How I wish Katie and I had a home!

The Abandoned Children's Toys Project (ACT) came about when the author was given an abandoned stuffed animal that once belonged to a child who could only bring one toy into the homeless shelter. We hope this story will inspire you to help homeless children and adults in your community. Please contact agencies that are sheltering the homeless to see what they need most. Here are three suggestions in the Detroit area:

COTS, The Coalition on Temporary Shelter
26 Peterboro Street
Detroit, Michigan 48201
313.831.3777
www.cotsdetroit.org/

Cass Community Social Services
313.883.2277
www.casscommunity.org

SOS, South Oakland Shelter
431 N. Main Street
Royal Oak, Michigan 48067
248.546.6566

ACT ~ Abandoned Children's Toys Project

Fund Raising Idea for Schools and Churches

1. Read this book, Only One Toy Allowed, and discuss the facts about homelessness.
2. Post flyers advertising a Used Toy Sale.
3. Have the children bring in used toys, books and games that they no longer use.
4. After a collection period, have the used toy sale.
5. Send the proceeds from the sale to a local shelter of your choice.
6. Find a new home for this story and give the book to another school or church to help this cause.

Facts About Homelessness

- Homeless families with children have increased significantly over the past decade. 1% of the U.S. population experiences homelessness each year. (Urban Institute, 2000)
- 3.5 million persons, 1.35 million of them children are likely to experience homelessness in a given year. (National Center on Homelessness and Poverty, 2007)
- In 2004, children under the age of 18 accounted for 39% of the homeless population and 42% of those children were under 5. (National Law Center on Homelessness and Poverty, 2004)
- Some reasons for homelessness are: prolonged unemployment, sudden loss of job, lack of affordable housing, domestic violence, etc.
- Many people will not be counted as homeless because they stay in automobiles, campgrounds, tents, boxes, etc. These people are called the "unsheltered" or "hidden" homeless.
- Nationally, 1 in 5 homeless persons is employed. (National Coalition for the Homeless)
- On an average night in Detroit, more than 9,500 individuals and families are homeless. However, only 1,995 shelter beds exist to serve the population. (Wayne State University, Research Group on Homelessness and Poverty, Dr. Paul Toro, 2002)

To learn more about homelessness, please go to these links:

National Coalition for the Homeless: www.nationalhomeless.org/
National Alliance to End Homelessness: www.endhomelessness.org/
National Law Center on Homelessness and Poverty: www.nlchp.org/
Research Group on Homelessness and Poverty: http://sun.science.wayne.edu/~ptoro/
National Low Income Housing Coalition: www.nlihc.org/
Michigan Coalition Against Homelessness: www.mihomeless.org/